THE AMAZING SPIDER-MAN

MEGATRON™

DECEPTICON

Hasbro. All Rights Reserved.

www.harpercollinschildrens.com
Library of Congress catalog card number: 2008928095
ISBN 978-0-06-162626-5

Book design by John Sazaklis
❖
First Edition

PROLOGUE

PETER PARKER WAS JUST AN ORDINARY HIGH SCHOOL STUDENT—UNTIL HE WAS BITTEN BY A RADIOACTIVE SPIDER AND HIS LIFE CHANGED COMPLETELY. PETER DEVELOPED SUPERHUMAN STRENGTH AND A POWERFUL INNER SENSE THAT PROVIDED HIM WITH EARLY WARNING OF DANGER. LIKE A SPIDER, HE COULD CLING TO MOST SURFACES, CRAWL OVER WALLS, AND SHOOT WEBS.

PETER PARKER HAD BECOME . . .

THE AMAZING SPIDER-MAN

CHAPTER 1

DING-A-LING-A-LING! DING-A-LING-A-LING!

The bell from an ice cream truck rang out loudly.

"Last one to the ice cream truck is a melted sundae!" Walter Hardy shouted, before dashing toward the street.

"Not fair, Daddy!" his thirteen-year-old daughter, Felicia, cried out. She leaped off the swing in their backyard and raced after her father. "You got a head start!"

As Felicia and her dad shared a giant ice cream sundae, the young girl's mood began to darken. She loved her dad and loved every minute they were able to spend together.

But Walter Hardy was a traveling salesman. He spent a lot of time on the road. Felicia always felt sad and angry when he was gone. And tomorrow morning he was leaving on another long trip that would keep them apart for weeks. Right now, she wished the ice cream sundae would last forever.

When Walter had eaten the last spoonful, he turned and made his way toward the house. "I have to pack, sweetheart," he said. "I'm off on the road early tomorrow morning."

"I know," Felicia said sadly.

"But I'll be back soon and I'll bring you a special present!" Walter said, trying to lift his daughter's spirits.

"Really special?" she asked, unable to hold back a smile.

"Super-duper, out-of-this-world special with a cherry on top!" her father replied. "Just like that sundae."

"Oh, Daddy," she said. "Sometimes you are so corny!" Then she laughed and ran after him.

On the day her father was due back, Felicia rushed home after school.

"Mom!" she shouted. "Is he here yet?"

"He's, um, going to be on the road a little longer this time, dear," her mother replied.

"Is everything all right, Mom?" Felicia asked when she saw the expression on her mother's face.

"Sure," her mom said. "Everything's fine." Then she quickly turned away.

The next morning, as Felicia dashed from the house to make the school bus, she stumbled over the folded copy of the *Daily Bugle* newspaper that sat on the front step. The paper fell open, and Felicia was stunned by what she saw. There was a photo of her beloved father being led away by the police in handcuffs! The huge headline read: NOTORIOUS CAT BURGLAR FINALLY CAUGHT!

CHAPTER 2

"YOU'VE BEEN LYING TO ME for years!" Felicia shouted at her mother. She slammed the newspaper down on the kitchen table. "Why didn't you tell me the truth about Dad?"

Her mother started sobbing. "I wanted to protect you. I never wanted you to get involved with that part of his life. He loves you, and that's all you need to know."

Felicia ran from the house. Her mind raced. She was shocked to learn that her father was a criminal, yet she still loved him so much. She was also curious about what exactly a cat burglar did. She couldn't believe that her father would ever hurt anybody.

Rushing to the library, she began to research her father's life. She searched through old newspapers. The more she learned, the more interested she became.

Felicia discovered that she was right. Her father had never hurt anyone. He hadn't needed to. She learned that her father was a skilled acrobat who could climb up the sides of buildings. He was an expert lock picker and was skilled at cracking open even the most secure safes. He could move silently through the night. He could get in and out of a building so fast that he could rob it before anyone even knew he was there.

Felicia admired her father's skill and cleverness. Right then and there, she decided to take up where he had left off. Felicia Hardy would train herself to become the world's greatest cat burglar.

Over the next few years, Felicia worked hard. She learned martial arts and gymnastics. She built her strength and agility. She practiced picking locks, opening safes, and climbing up the outsides of buildings. When she felt she was ready to step into her father's shoes, she put on a costume to hide her identity. Felicia Hardy became Black Cat.

Although she had no superpowers, Felicia cleverly designed tricks to make people believe that she had the

Felicia Hardy became Black Cat.

ability to jinx them with bad luck—just like a real black cat. She planned ahead to set up her tricks in advance, using wires and remote control devices. So if the police, for example, were chasing her, objects would fall, blocking their path. Walls would crumble, or doorknobs would suddenly snap off after she had left a room. Pipes would mysteriously burst, flooding an area.

All of these tricks would allow her to make her escapes. In each case, it would appear that the police had simply run into a bit of bad luck.

Felicia slipped into her jet-black costume and put on her mask. She knew exactly what her first adventure as Black Cat was going to be. She was going to break her father out of prison.

CHAPTER 3

SPIDER-MAN SWUNG THROUGH THE AIR high above the streets of New York City. A red and blue blur, Spidey was on his way home.

I barely survived my little run-in with Venom and Carnage, he thought, as he fired another strand from his web-shooter. The web stuck to a nearby building and supported his weight as he swung. *I need about a weeklong nap, but I'll settle for an hour before I have to deliver photos to the Daily Bugle as Peter Parker. Oh, and I still owe Dr. Connors that research project at school. What do they say? "No rest for the weary" . . . or the crime stopper, I guess. Still I—*

Whoa! Spider-sense just went wild, but I don't see any—

At that second, Spider-Man glanced up. He saw a figure dressed in black swinging on a cable above him.

"Hey, lady!" he shouted to the blonde-haired, masked woman. "Swinging above the city is *my* act. Find your own routine! Besides, if it gets any more crowded up here, I'm going to have to call a traffic cop."

Ignoring him, the mysterious woman released the cable. She did a somersault in midair. Then she fired a grappling hook at a nearby building. The sharp metal hook dug into the building's bricks, attaching itself securely. Connected to the hook was another thin, but strong, cable.

As Black Cat swung on the cable, the hook supported her weight. Using her hooks and cables in the same way Spider-Man used his webbing, she swung quickly through the city.

She's not bad, Spidey admitted to himself. *Great gymnastic moves, excellent form. I'd give her a 9.5. Still, something tells me she's not up here to get a better view of the traffic jam on Fifth Avenue. Better follow her and find out what she's up to.*

Web-slinging his way across town, Spider-Man followed the mysterious woman. She soon arrived at the city prison.

What's she doing here? Spidey wondered, as he stuck to the outside wall of the prison. *I'm guessing she's not here to put on a gymnastics show for the inmates.*

Spider-Man's spider-sense began to tingle again. *Above me!* he thought. Just as he looked up, the woman he had been following slammed into his back, feetfirst. Spider-Man tumbled forward and plunged toward the pavement below.

Firing a web-line onto the building, he stopped his fall just inches above the ground. Looking up, he saw the mystery woman climbing straight up the wall.

Now she's wall-crawling, too! he thought. *I'm flattered that she likes my moves, but this town is only big enough for one wall-crawler!*

"Hey!" Spider-Man shouted. "Who are you?"

"Sorry, web-head, but I'm a little busy at the moment," the woman yelled back. "The formal introductions will have to wait. But for the record, you can call me Black Cat.

Spider-Man plunged toward the pavement below.

And you know what they say about black cats—we're bad luck!"

Spider-Man followed her up the side of the prison. "Nice running into you, Black Cat," Spidey called out, rubbing his sore back. "Or should I say, 'running into me.'" *What is she doing?* he thought. *Breaking* into *prison? Who does that?*

THOOM!

The entire building shook as an explosion went off inside the prison. The force of the blast knocked Spider-Man off the building. Somersaulting, he flipped himself back onto the wall, sticking there by his hands and feet.

That explosion was inside the prison, Spider-Man realized. *She's not breaking in, she's breaking someone out! But who?*

The answer to Spidey's question came in the form of a huge man who suddenly appeared on the prison's roof.

So she's not working alone! She has help—rather large help!

Slung over the enormous man's shoulder was an older man. The muscle man tossed a rope over the roof's edge.

Then he began scrambling down the rope, carrying the older man.

Spider-Man fired a web and swung up toward the roof. "Gee, Cat, I hate to break up this little party. But there's one minor problem with you breaking someone out of prison—it's against the law!"

"Hey, you want me to squash the bug?" the large man called out to Black Cat. He scowled at Spider-Man.

"No!" she shouted back. "Get Father out of here. I'll deal with Spider-Man."

Father? Spidey thought. *She just broke her father out of prison. That's a new one.*

Spider-Man swung up toward the huge man. "Sorry, big guy, but if there's any squashing to be done around here, it's going to be me squashing your little prison break."

Spidey landed on the wall beside the muscle man. Suddenly, the section of wall Spider-Man was on began to crumble and he tumbled to the ground. Spider-Man landed hard, with a large mound of bricks falling on top of him. Struggling, he poked his head out from the heavy pile of rubble. Black Cat was leaning over him.

"Looks like you've run into some of that bad luck I warned you about," she said. "Well, here's my next piece of advice: Never let a Black Cat cross your path!"

Then she disappeared from view.

CHAPTER 4

USING HIS SPIDER-STRENGTH, SPIDER-MAN crawled out from under the rubble.

That was a lucky break for Black Cat, Spider-Man thought, as he brushed himself off. *And some bad luck for me. If that wall hadn't crumbled just then, I would have stopped her. Now I've got to track her down.*

Spider-Man swung across the city, looking for Black Cat. His body ached and his mind still felt fuzzy as he scanned block after block. There was no sign of Black Cat. Then he remembered his deadline.

I've got to get those photos to Jameson, he thought as he headed home. *I'll have to pick up the search for Black Cat later.*

Back in his apartment, Spider-Man pulled off his costume, took a quick shower, and got dressed in his regular clothes. Grabbing his camera and a stack of photos he had taken, he raced out the door.

"Jameson's going to give me grief for being so late with these shots," he muttered to himself as he hurried to the offices of the *Daily Bugle*. "So what else is new!"

Bursting into the office of J. Jonah Jameson, publisher of the *Daily Bugle*, Peter found his boss screaming into the phone.

"I don't want excuses, I want stories!" Jameson shouted. "What? Your car broke down? Well, you still have legs, don't you? Good—use them!" Then he slammed the phone down and looked up, scowling at Peter.

"Parker!" Jameson screamed. "You're late! But why should I be surprised? Why should I expect my photographer to actually give me photos in time to run them in the newspaper? You do remember that we're running a newspaper here, Parker?"

"Mr. Jameson, I—"

"Don't interrupt me when I'm screaming at

you, Parker! Now, I want those photos on my desk immediately!"

"Yes, sir," Peter said softly, placing the stack of photos onto Jameson's desk.

"What are these?" Jameson blustered.

"The photos," Peter replied.

"Right!" Jameson shouted back. "Now get out of my office!"

Well, Jameson is his usual cheery self, Peter thought as he left his boss's office. As he headed down the hall, he heard a commotion at the *Bugle*'s city news desk. "What's going on?" he asked the city editor.

"Just got this over the police scanner," the editor replied. "There's a robbery in progress at the sculpture museum. Some weirdo dressed in black with a mask and big claws!"

Black Cat! Peter thought as he dashed from the building. *She didn't wait long to strike again. Got to stop her. Only this time I hope I don't run into any bad luck!*

CHAPTER 5

PETER CHANGED INTO HIS SPIDER-MAN suit and swung swiftly toward the museum. When he arrived, Spidey spotted police cars surrounding the building.

Best to go in through the roof, he thought. *No need to draw attention to myself. Besides, the cops tend to view all us costumed weirdoes as bad guys.*

Dropping down onto the museum's roof, Spider-Man crawled down a wall and slipped into the building through a window. He looked down from the high ceiling and saw Black Cat grabbing a gold statue.

The famous Golden Couple statue! I read about that in the Bugle. *What does she want with that?* he wondered.

Spider-Man lowered himself down on a web. He paused just above Black Cat.

"I'm sorry, miss, but the museum's closed."

"I'm sorry, miss, but the museum's closed," he quipped. "Unless, of course, you have a membership card."

"Spider-Man!" Black Cat cried. "You again!"

"In the flesh!" he replied, reaching down and grabbing her wrist. "Did you miss me?"

Black Cat whipped her arm forward and flipped Spider-Man over her shoulder. He tumbled through the air and landed on his feet.

"I'll take that as a no," he said, turning to face her. "By the way, nice judo move. You're just full of tricks, aren't you?"

"You haven't seen anything yet, web-head," Black Cat said. "Unfortunately, right now I have to run. Bye!"

Black Cat turned and ran, clutching the statue under her arm. She jumped onto the top of a huge display case filled with precious pottery.

"I'm afraid this is one time a cat won't be able to outrun a spider," Spider-Man quipped. "Or at least a spider's webbing."

He fired a web-line across the room. It stuck to the statue. Pulling back on his webbing, Spider-Man yanked the golden treasure free. The statue zoomed across the room and landed in his waiting hands.

"Return the statue to its rightful place here in the museum?" Spider-Man said. "What a good idea, Cat. See, I knew there was something I liked about you."

Spider-Man turned to place the statue back onto its stand. Black Cat spun toward him, cartwheeling feet over head. Then, leaping into the air and wrapping her arms around her knees, she slammed into Spider-Man like a cannonball.

Spider-Man flew across the room, still holding the statue firmly in his hands. He landed on the far wall, his feet sticking there.

Black Cat applauded slowly. "Oh, you are good," she said. "No wonder I'm your biggest fan."

"If this is how you treat a fellow costumed oddball, I'd hate to see how you treat someone you *don't* like," Spider-Man said.

"Yes, you would hate it," Black Cat agreed. "But I can't stick around to chat about it. I'm a little short on time and you have something I need."

"I think the folks here at the museum need it more," Spidey pointed out. He fired his webbing toward the ceiling, and then swung across the room and placed the statue back onto its stand.

"Remember what I said about crossing my path!" Black Cat said, smiling.

"Sorry, Cat, but I don't believe in bad lu—"

Spider-Man's spider-sense kicked into high gear, warning him of danger. Spinning around, he spotted the huge display case filled with precious pottery toppling over. The glass door to the case swung wide open, and pottery began to tumble out.

That's precious ancient pottery! Spider-Man thought. *I can't let it hit the ground!*

"Better hurry, web-head," Black Cat said. "Those are priceless pieces of art from the ninth century. Looks like the museum has just run into a bit of bad luck. Oh, but that's right, you don't believe in bad luck, do you?"

Firing a web, Spider-Man swung across the room. He caught two small ceramic pots just before they hit the floor. Then he landed, turned, and grabbed a huge falling vase.

Cradling the precious pottery in his arms, he dived out of the way. The empty display case crashed to the floor.

Spider-Man placed the pottery gently down. Then he looked up to discover that Black Cat had vanished—along with the golden statue.

Another convenient accident, Spider-Man thought as he swung back up to the ceiling. *And again, Black Cat got away because of it. Every time I'm about to stop her, something bad happens. I've battled lots of costumed crazies with all kinds of superpowers. But could this one really have the ability to bring bad luck?*

Reaching the roof, Spider-Man found no trace of Black Cat.

Nice going, Spidey! You let yourself get outfoxed— by a cat!

CHAPTER 6

THE FOLLOWING DAY, SPIDER-MAN SCALED the side of a tall building. Using his sticky webbing, he attached his camera to the building and set the automatic timer.

Jameson's been screaming at me for some new pictures of Spidey in action, he thought. *Good thing I didn't set my camera up before my battle with Black Cat—although Jameson would probably love some shots of Spidey getting outsmarted by a supervillain. But that wouldn't do much for Spider-Man's reputation. I think a few spectacular web-slinging shots should do the trick, though.*

Spidey fired a web-line over to a nearby rooftop and swung out into the street. The camera automatically took shot after shot of his amazing acrobatics. He swooped past the camera, again and again.

I have to make these look unposed. That'll earn extra brownie points for Peter Parker. I'll just—

Suddenly, his spider-sense began tingling like mad.

There! he thought. *Below on the street. People screaming and running.*

Spider-Man swung down toward the street. *The panic seems to be around that jewelry store.*

KA-RASH!

The jewelry store's window exploded outward. The startled crowd dived for cover. Suddenly, Black Cat appeared, jumping through the cloud of shattered glass. She fired a grappling hook from a wrist-mounted launcher. The hook streaked through the air and attached itself to a nearby building. Black Cat swung away from the store on a cable attached to the hook.

"Somebody stop her!" the owner of the jewelry store shouted. "She stole the Love Ruby. It's worth millions!"

"I have to give you credit, Cat," Spider-Man shouted, as he swung after the fleeing thief. "You've got good taste. Unfortunately, you also have this problem with a little thing that I like to call obeying the law!"

"Why is it you keep turning up wherever I am, Spider-Man?" Black Cat called back. "Are you trying to become my friend or something?"

"Most of my friends pay for the things they take out of stores," Spidey replied.

Spider-Man caught up to Black Cat. She turned to face him.

Is she giving up? he wondered.

Snik!

Long claws suddenly extended from Black Cat's gloves. With a rapid slicing motion, she cut right through Spider-Man's webbing. He tumbled downward.

"More bad luck, I'm afraid!" Black Cat called down to him. Then she pulled her claws back in.

I guess she's not giving up, Spidey thought, as he fired another strand of webbing to stop his fall. *Then again, neither am I.*

Black Cat dropped down onto a rooftop, landing beside a water tower. Spider-Man followed, but when he reached the roof, he saw no sign of her.

"I know cats can sometimes be coy," Spidey called

out. "But you just don't strike me as the shy type."

At that moment Black Cat appeared near the top of the water tower. Displaying great gymnastic skill, she made her way to the upper portion of the tower. Then she vanished again.

"Are we playing a little game of cat and mouse?" Spider-Man asked. "Or should I say, cat and spider?"

Black Cat appeared again, this time sliding down one of the tower's legs.

"What have you been doing up on that water tower?" Spidey asked. "If you're thirsty, I can put out a saucer of milk."

"The only thing I'm thirsty for is this lovely little ruby," Black Cat replied, holding up the gem she had stolen. "It just said, 'Take me,' so I did."

"That's funny," Spider-Man replied. "What it says to me is ten to fifteen years behind bars for the thief who stole it. But then again, you and I don't seem to speak the same language, do we?"

"Well, see if you understand this, web-head," Black Cat said. "Bye!"

Without another word, Black Cat vaulted over the edge of the rooftop. Spider-Man dashed across the roof and peered over.

Moving with incredible speed, Black Cat swung herself back up toward the roof. She sailed over Spider-Man's head and landed behind him. Then she grabbed him around the waist and launched herself into a backward somersault. As she rolled back, she tossed Spidey over her head.

"You never seem to learn, do you?" Black Cat said, landing back up on her feet. "Bad luck just follows me around."

Spider-Man sailed headfirst through the air, spinning. He landed upright and then fired a strand of webbing at the ruby, which Black Cat still held tightly in her fist. As she ducked out of the way, the webbing shot right past her.

"You continue to impress, Cat," Spidey said. "Too bad you use your skills for the wrong things."

"Uh-oh, do I sense a lecture coming up?" Black Cat said, slowly edging toward the far end of the roof.

"Because I forgot my notepad and my laptop's in the shop. Besides, I hate lectures. And so . . . class dismissed!"

Spider-Man's spider-sense began tingling. He heard a loud crack and turned in the direction of the sound. To his horror, he saw that one of the wooden legs of the water tower had split in half. The enormous tower, filled with thousands of gallons of water, was now toppling over.

CHAPTER 7

THAT TOWER IS GOING TO fall off the roof, onto the crowded street below! Spider-Man thought.

He fired webbing from each hand. The powerful webs struck the falling tower. As Spider-Man pulled hard on the webbing, the tower stopped tumbling.

So heavy, he thought, as he struggled with all his spider-strength to hold up the tower. Stepping back, he attached the end of his webbing to a brick chimney, and then let go.

"It worked!" he cried "That should hold it up and—"

The chimney began to shift and crack, unable to support the weight of the water tower.

"Or not!" he said, dashing to the tower, which was

Bad luck for me, good luck for her.

again moving toward the edge of the roof and straining Spidey's webbing to its limit.

SNAP! The webbing broke.

Balancing himself on the edge of the roof, Spider-Man reached up and caught the tower. His knees buckled and his back arched.

I'll get only one shot at this, he thought. Pushing up, Spider-Man gave the tower a mighty shove. It creaked back up into position.

Spidey then quickly attached another web-line from the tower to the roof itself. *This should buy me a few seconds.*

He picked up the broken wooden leg and set it back into position. Then he fired a thick glob of sticky webbing right onto the spot where the leg had snapped. *This will have to do, since I'm fresh out of Krazy Glue!*

The tower stood in place. "I hope that does the trick for now," he said, catching his breath. "Of course, the Cat used that perfectly timed bit of bad luck to make her getaway—again!"

Black Cat does seem to have the power to produce bad luck. Bad luck for me, that is. Good luck for her.

CHAPTER 8

THE NEXT MORNING, PETER PARKER rushed into Jonah
Jameson's office.

"Here you go, Mr. Jameson," Peter said, tossing a
stack of photos onto his boss's desk. "Brand-new shots of
Spider-Man in action."

"What do I want these for, Parker?" Jameson shouted,
flipping through the shots. "Spider-Man is last week's news.
And do you know who buys a newspaper that prints last
week's news? Nobody! That's who!"

"But you asked—"

"Go get me a great shot of that new costumed nut
who's been running around town!" Jameson interrupted.
"What's her name? Black Claw? Brown Cat?"

"Black Cat?!" Peter exclaimed.

"Bingo! Black Cat. You win the prize, Parker. So why are you still standing here? Go get me a shot of this Cat and I might even pay you. Now—"

"I know," Peter sighed. "Get out of your office."

Great! Peter thought, as he left Jameson's office. *Now not only does Spider-Man have a reason to find Black Cat, but Peter Parker does, too. She has always been one step ahead of me. If I can just figure out where she'll strike next. . . . Let's see, everything she's taken so far has had a love theme—the Golden Couple statue, the Love Ruby—and are high profile in the news. That gives me an idea!*

Peter grabbed a copy of the latest edition of the *Bugle*. Flipping through the paper, his eyes opened wide when he got to the listings of upcoming openings of art exhibits. He read aloud: "World-famous painting *Love in the Springtime* will make its New York City debut at the Museum of Modern Art tomorrow. The painting will be shown in the museum's main gallery."

How could the Cat possibly resist Love in the Springtime? *She'll be there. I'm sure of it. And this time I'll be ready!*

As Peter hurried from the *Daily Bugle* building, his cell phone started beeping.

Voice mail, he thought. *Who left me a message?*

Checking his voice mail, Peter heard a message from Dr. Curtis Connors, his science professor at Empire State University. Peter, a brilliant science student, had been helping Dr. Connors with a research project.

"Oh, great!" Peter grumbled, when he had finished listening to the message. "Dr. Connors wants the project on his desk first thing tomorrow morning. But the museum opens at ten in the morning, and I need to move bright and early if I'm going to catch Black Cat. Looks like it's gonna be an all-nighter. Better pick up some extra coffee!"

Peter worked through the night finishing his project for Dr. Connors. He even managed to grab two hours of sleep before rushing off to the campus lab, where he delivered his work early the next morning.

"Excellent work as usual, Peter," Dr. Connors said, as he looked through the research paper. "But why do you always leave everything until the last minute? You have the makings of a great scientist. You've got a terrific mind, but your work habits need to improve. One of these days you'll stop rushing from place to place and focus on what's really important."

"Yes, sir," Peter said, glancing up at the clock.

"There you go again, looking at the clock," Dr. Connors said. "I suppose you have somewhere you need to be."

Actually I have somewhere Spider-Man needs to be, Peter thought. "I do," he said, rushing to the door. "Sorry, Dr. Connors. I have to go."

"Go, go!" the professor said, shaking his head. "Although I can't imagine what could possibly be more interesting than chemistry!"

Well, catching Black Cat for a start! Peter thought. He dashed up to the lab's roof and changed into his Spider-Man costume. Taking to the rooftops, he swung his way across the city as fast as he could move.

CHAPTER 9

ARRIVING AT THE MUSEUM OF Modern Art a few minutes later, Spider-Man spotted a long line of people waiting to get in to see *Love in the Springtime*.

Usually I follow the rules, he thought, as he crawled up the back wall of the museum. *But today I'm afraid I don't have the time to wait in line like everyone else.* When he reached the window to the museum's main gallery, Spidey slipped inside.

There, he saw two police officers. *Hmm, it's strange for the police to be here, he thought. Maybe they're concerned about extra security for this super valuable painting.*

Spider-Man crawled silently along the back wall of the gallery. He saw a sign that read *Love in the Springtime* next to a large curtain.

They're keeping the painting behind a curtain. Very classy. I'll just slip back there and wait for the Cat to show up.

Keeping himself hidden from the police officers, Spider-Man ducked behind the curtain.

Now, let's have a look at—gone! The painting is gone! So that's why the cops are here. Black Cat must have taken it already. She's even quicker than I thought.

Spider-Man peered around the curtain and was stunned to see Black Cat sneaking into the gallery. She climbed through the same window Spidey had used to get in.

This doesn't make any sense, Spider-Man thought. *Why would she come back if she'd already taken the painting? Unless . . . someone else beat her to it! She doesn't know it's already gone!*

Black Cat leaped up onto a giant chandelier that hung from the ceiling.

"Look!" shouted one of the officers. "It's that cat burglar who's been stealing art across the city!"

"Black Cat's the name," she announced.

"If you're here for *Love in the Springtime,* you're too

late!" growled the other officer.

"As a matter of fact, gentlemen, I'm early," Black Cat replied. "I jumped to the head of the line."

She swung on the chandelier, using it like a trapeze. Then she let go, dropping to the ground.

The police officers rushed toward her.

Just as they reached her, Black Cat jumped toward a nearby wall. Then, springing off the wall, she landed behind them.

Tucking herself into a tight ball, Black Cat tumbled toward the officers. Like a bowling ball crashing into pins, she knocked their legs out from under them. Then she quickly pulled out some rope she had attached to her costume and tied them up to a nearby column.

"And now for a glimpse at the masterpiece," she said, rushing to the exhibit.

Black Cat threw open the curtain. There, dangling upside down, hung Spider-Man.

"Well, I have to say, I've been called many things in my life, but never a 'masterpiece,'" Spider-Man said. "I'm so touched. In fact, under the mask, I'm blushing!"

"Spider-Man!" Black Cat shouted. "What are you doing here?"

"What? You think you're the only art lover who runs around in a funny costume?" Spidey replied, dropping to his feet.

"Where's the painting?" Black Cat asked, noticing the blank wall behind Spidey.

"That seems to be exactly what the cops you so rudely tied up were trying to figure out," Spider-Man explained. "It seems that someone beat us both to the punch and snatched the painting in the middle of the night."

"Too bad," Black Cat hissed. "But, rather than stick around to get arrested, I'll just be going."

With amazing speed, Black Cat began climbing back up her cable toward the window.

"Not so fast, kitty," Spidey said, firing a web-line and swinging up after her.

As Spider-Man approached, Black Cat swung her cable toward him. Slamming into him with her shoulder, she knocked Spidey off his webbing. He tumbled away, but reached up and grabbed her ankle to stop his fall.

"Not so fast, kitty."

Swinging himself up feetfirst, Spider-Man landed on Black Cat's cable, just above her head.

"While you're really fun to hang around with, Cat, I think we should both get down and talk," Spidey said. "We can do that the easy way or the hard way."

"Don't you know by now that I always prefer the hard way?" Black Cat replied. "The hard *luck* way!"

SNAP!

The chain that had been holding the chandelier in the middle of the ceiling broke in half. The huge light plunged down, heading right for a glass display of ceramic artifacts.

Got to stop that thing before it lands! Spider-Man thought, leaping from the cable. He fired a thick strand of webbing back up to the ceiling and held on to it firmly with one hand. With his other hand, Spidey snatched the chandelier's chain. It jerked to a stop—just inches above the display case.

Swinging slightly to the side, Spider-Man gently placed the chandelier on the ground.

"I thought you were here to steal the painting, too!"

said one of the police officers, as Spider-Man the men.

"Me?" Spidey said in shock. "You got me all wrong. I'm one of the good guys."

"Then what were you doing sneaking into the museum?" asked one of the officers.

"I came to catch a cat," Spider-Man explained. "And to untie you. Do you know who took the painting?"

"We're working on it," said the police officer. "So far all the clues point to Phil Bradshaw."

"The mob boss?" Spidey asked.

"Yeah, he's been into stealing art and jewels lately," the police officer replied.

"Sounds like someone else I know," Spidey muttered. "Well, be careful. And don't let any more black cats cross your path!" Then Spider-Man swung up to the window and slipped out.

Okay, Spider-Man thought, as he swung away from the museum. *There's definitely a pattern here. Every one of these so-called bad luck accidents happened after Black Cat was on or near whatever went wrong. She was on the scene when the chandelier fell, when the leg broke on the water tower, and*

when the display case toppled inside the museum. Does she really have the power of bad luck? Or is she just playing me for a fool?

Well, at least this day wasn't a total loss. I did manage to stick a spider-tracer onto Black Cat's ankle during that last run-in. So now I can follow her. And my spider-sense is already picking up the signal. Time to pay the Cat a little visit—at home!

SPIDER-MAN FOLLOWED THE SPIDER-TRACER SIGNAL to a small apartment building. Landing on a window ledge and keeping out of sight, he looked through the window.

Spider-Man saw Black Cat inside the apartment, polishing the statue of the Golden Couple. She placed it beside the Love Ruby she had taken.

"Nice collection," Spider-Man said, slipping though the window into the apartment. "Too bad it belongs to someone else."

Black Cat spun around, startled by Spider-Man's sudden appearance. Although she was still wearing her costume, she had removed her mask. For the first time, Spider-Man saw her face.

"How did you find me?" she asked nervously.

"A little good luck," Spidey replied, "Felicia."

"You know my name," she said, more nervous than Spider-Man had ever seen her.

"It didn't take much research to figure out that the daughter of Walter Hardy, one of the world's greatest cat burglars, was the one trying to pick up where dear old dad left off," Spider-Man explained.

That's when Spider-Man took his first good look around the room. Plastered on every wall were posters, photos, and newspaper clippings—all about him!

"What's up with all this, Felicia?" he asked, a bit stunned. "Not that I object to your taste in Super Heroes, but . . ."

Felicia looked away shyly. "I've been a huge fan of yours for years," she explained. "And lately I've developed a bit of a crush on you, I guess. Sounds pretty dumb when I say it to your face now, huh?" she said. "Now I just hope we can at least be friends."

"My friends aren't usually lawbreakers," Spidey pointed out. "In fact, I'd probably put that one at the top

of the list of the worst ways of becoming my friend."

Felicia looked away, embarrassed.

"I'd say the best way would be to give up your life of crime and return the things you stole," he continued. "All your skill and talent could be put to way better use."

"But my father," she said quickly. "I wanted to honor him, once I found out the truth about him. Once he went away to jail, I lost him. And now, even after I busted him out, the police tracked him down and returned him to prison."

"Your father made his choices. He led his own life," Spider-Man explained. "And you're free to do the same. I know what it's like to lose a father."

His thoughts turned, as they did every day, to his Uncle Ben. Uncle Ben had raised him as a father would have. He thought again of the fateful night when his uncle's life was taken by a thief Peter could have easily stopped—but didn't.

"I learned a painful lesson when I lost the man who had raised me," Spider-Man continued. "I learned that with great power comes great responsibility. You've got amazing powers, Felicia. It's up to you to use them for the right things."

"Like what?" Felicia asked, growing more interested.

"Like joining me," he replied. "I think we'd make a great team. With my spider-powers and your catlike abilities, who could stop us? By the way, how does that whole bad luck thing work? Could you teach me?"

"I don't really have any superpowers," Felicia admitted. "I worked hard on the gymnastics for years. And the bad luck stuff . . . well, I rigged all those things to make it look like I could control bad luck. The prison wall, the museum shelves, the water tower, the chandelier. I set them all up in advance. Then I used a remote control device to knock them over or break them. You might say I gave my bad luck a little helping hand."

Snik!

Her electro-claws sprang out from her gloves. "These I had specially made. After all, a cat needs her claws."

"Must be nice to be able to afford all those gadgets

and tricks," Spider-Man said. "I still have to whip up my web fluid using leftovers from my high school chemistry set."

"Maybe I can loan you a few new tricks," Felicia offered.

"So does this mean we're a team?" Spidey asked.

"We're a team," she replied, slipping her mask back on. "What's our first job?"

"Once you return the statue and the ruby, you're going to help me rescue *Love in the Springtime* and return it to the museum!"

CHAPTER 11

LATER THAT EVENING, SPIDER-MAN AND Black Cat crouched on top of a fancy apartment building.

"Nice place," Black Cat commented. "I guess Phil Bradshaw can live wherever he likes."

"One of the benefits of being a ruthless mob boss," Spider-Man replied. "Maybe if the whole Super Hero thing doesn't work out for you, you can apply for the job."

"Can I use you as a reference?" she asked.

"Funny," Spidey said.

"So we're just going to crash Bradshaw's little costume party and steal back the painting?" Black Cat asked.

"That's the plan," Spider-Man replied.

"Not much of a plan, if you ask me," Black Cat commented.

"Hey, I think on my feet," Spidey quipped. "It's what I do."

"Why don't we just walk through the front door?" she asked. "We *are* wearing costumes, after all."

"That'll help us blend in once we're inside," Spider-Man explained. "But without a formal invitation, I don't think Bradshaw's goons would be too happy to see us. Come on. It's showtime!"

Spider-Man crawled down the side of the building. Black Cat followed, creeping along a cable she had fastened to the roof with a grappling hook. Silently slipping through an open window, they entered the party, which was already in full swing.

Gangsters dressed as clowns, lions, and aliens nibbled on food and sipped drinks.

"Nice costume, bub," a clown said, as Spider-Man walked past. "But I think the real Spider-Man is taller."

"He just looks that way in pictures," Spidey replied.

"Hey, lady," a court jester said to Black Cat. "What are you supposed to be, a black widow spider?"

Snik!

Black Cat extended her claws and brought them up

to the jester's face. "Spiders don't have claws, do they, funny guy?"

"Easy, Cat," Spider-Man whispered, steering her away. "The point here is to blend in, not to draw attention to ourselves."

Phil Bradshaw stepped to the front of the room. A curtain covered a small section of the wall behind him.

"Ladies and gentlemen," Bradshaw began in a loud, booming voice. "And the rest of you, too!"

The costumed crowd broke into laughter.

"I am so glad that all my close friends and business partners could be here for the unveiling of my latest piece of fine art," Bradshaw continued.

The crowd applauded.

"And now, without further ado, *Love in the Springtime!*"

Bradshaw pulled open the curtain, revealing the masterpiece he had stolen from the museum.

"That's our cue, Cat," Spidey whispered. "Get ready."

Spider-Man leaped onto the wall above the painting.

"Sorry to spoil the party, folks, but we'll just be

"That's our cue, Cat. Get ready."

returning that painting to the museum," he said.

"It's the real Spider-Man!" Bradshaw cried. "Get him, boys!"

A clown and an alien charged toward Spider-Man. He fired webbing in thick globs, which wrapped around the gangsters' hands. Yanking hard on his end of the webbing, Spidey sent the gangsters flying off their feet.

"And here's another surprise for you fine gents," Black Cat said, leaping in between two gangsters who were dressed as a pirate and an astronaut. "I'm the real Black Cat!"

Black Cat placed her hands onto the gangsters' shoulders. She vaulted forward, kicking her legs out, slamming two more gangsters to the ground. Landing, she turned back toward the pirate and the astronaut and cannonballed into their legs. They toppled to the ground.

"That's it!" Spider-Man shouted, when the last of the gangsters had been taken care of. "You grab the painting, I'll finish up here. Meet you on the roof!"

Black Cat snatched the painting off the wall and scrambled out the window.

Spider-Man created a giant net from his webbing. For a split second, he wondered if he was right in trusting the Cat with the painting. Joining her outside a few moments later, he got his answer.

"Worried I might take off with the goods again?" she asked, as if reading his mind.

"Me? No, no, no. Well, yes, a little," he said sheepishly. "After all, you're the one who told me never to trust a black cat."

"But that was before we became partners, partner," she pointed out.

"Not bad for our first job together," Spider-Man said. "Stick with me, kid, and you'll go far in the Super Hero business. At least far enough across town to return that painting to the museum."

A short while later, the police arrived at Phil Bradshaw's apartment. They found a bunch of costumed gangsters hanging from the ceiling in a large net made of spider-webbing. Attached to the net was a note that read: COMPLIMENTS OF YOUR FRIENDLY NEIGHBORHOOD SPIDER-MAN . . . AND BLACK CAT.

CHAPTER 12

"BETTER LET ME TAKE CARE of this," Spider-Man said to Black Cat. The two stood on the roof of the Museum of Modern Art. "They might not be too pleased to see you again. Come to think of it, I'm not the most popular guy around here, either. So I'll make this quick and quiet."

"Okay," Black Cat replied. "I have something I need to get, but I'll meet you right back here." Then she swung off the roof on her grappling cable.

Spider-Man slipped through a window. He eased himself down slowly on a web-line. *No one around,* he thought. *Perfect.* He dropped to the museum floor silently and rehung *Love in the Springtime* in its proper place. Then, just as quickly, he scrambled back up his webbing to the roof.

A few minutes later, Black Cat returned.

"I brought you something, partner," she said, handing Spider-Man a small metal device. "It's a little thing I like to call a Black Cat Comm-Link. I've got one, too. I thought that since we made such a good team you might like to call me again. And I hate giving out my cell phone number. All those annoying telemarketing calls, you know."

"Thanks," Spider-Man said. "Don't be surprised if you hear from me soon. Oh, before you go, there's one last thing you can do for me."

He pulled out his camera. "Smile! Perfect."

CLICK!

Jonah's gonna love this shot! Spider-Man thought. *It's got "front page" written all over it.*

"Thanks," he said, as the two went their separate ways. *And Peter Parker thanks you, too!*

ILLUSTRATION BY JOE F. MERKEL